# The Marvelous Mouse Man

## MARY ANN HOBERMAN

ILLUSTRATED BY
## LAURA FORMAN

GULLIVER BOOKS • HARCOURT, INC. • *San Diego   New York   London*

*For Linda Zuckerman, editor and friend*
—M. A. H.

*To Linda Zuckerman and Barbara Bottner, with gratitude*
—L. F.

www.harcourt.com

*Gulliver Books* is a trademark of Harcourt, Inc., registered in the United States of America and/or other jurisdictions.

Library of Congress Cataloging-in-Publication Data
Hoberman, Mary Ann.
The marvelous mouse man/by Mary Ann Hoberman; illustrated by Laura Forman.
p.   cm.
"Gulliver Books."
Summary: When the townsfolk hire a mysterious man to purge the village of mice,
he gets rid of too many other things as well.
[1. Mice—Fiction.  2. Stories in rhyme.]  I. Forman, Laura, ill.  II. Title.
PZ8.3.H66Mar   2002
[E]—dc21      98-11930
ISBN 0-15-201715-1

First edition
A C E G H F D B
Printed in Singapore

The illustrations in this book were done in pencil and
Dr. Ph. Martin's watercolor dyes on 140 lb. Arches watercolor paper.
The display type was set in Centaur Italic.
The text type was set in Bembo.
Color separations by Colourscan Co. Pte. Ltd., Singapore
Printed and bound by Tien Wah Press, Singapore
This book was printed on totally chlorine-free Nymolla Matte Art paper.
Production supervision by Sandra Grebenar and Ginger Boyer
Designed by Linda Lockowitz

Now settle down and listen well
To what I am about to tell
About the troubles that befell
    A town and set it spinning.
As such tales do, it started small,
With one wee mouse, just one, that's all,
Who one spring day came by to call—
    And that was the beginning.

Now one small mouse is always sweet,
With twitching nose and tiny feet,
And if you meet one in the street,
    Why, nothing is more pleasant.
And two or three are fine as well
If they should visit for a spell.
Why, even four do not repel
    Whenever they are present.

But when the welcome mat extends
And one by one they bring their friends,
At some point, sir, your patience ends
    And you become unhappy;
And when, no matter what you say,
They simply will not go away
And soon have settled in to stay,
    Your temper grows quite snappy.

I tell you, sir, it was not nice.
This town was soon aswarm with mice.
You need not look but once or twice
   To see them frisk and frolic
Till not a single store or house
Was uninvaded by a mouse
And every husband and his spouse
   Was rendered melancholic.

And that, sir, was what happened here.
Where'er you turned, a mouse was near,
Atop your head, behind your ear,
   Each time you put your hat on.
You had to peer inside your cup
For fear that you might drink one up,
And when you did sit down to sup
   A mouse was often sat on!

"What shall we do?" the townsfolk cried.
"In spite of everything we've tried,
They've covered all the countryside
    And still they keep on coming!
Their manners are extremely rude;
They don't show any gratitude;
And yet they gobble up our food
    And clog up all the plumbing!"

It wasn't long before the fame
Of "Mousy Town" (its brand-new name)
Had spread, and many strangers came
    To see the situation.
And there before their very eyes,
And far more numerous than flies,
Were mice of every shape and size
    In every odd location.

As into town the strangers poured,
The mayor came out to greet the horde
And offer up a large reward
    To anyone so clever
As to invent a new device,
No matter what its kind or price,
To rid the town of all its mice
    And banish them forever.

*T*hen from the crowd there stepped a man,
And straight up to the mayor he ran.
He said, "I have the very plan
   To solve your irksome worry.
If you will hire me today
And pay the sum you say you'll pay,
Your mice will soon be far away.
   I'll do it in a hurry.

"My skill has gained me great renown
And so I go from town to town
And though I'd like to settle down
   In some nearby location,
I've heard about your dreadful fix
And so I've brought my bag of tricks
From which I'll make the proper mix
   To ease your situation."

The man was very tall and thin
With wispy whiskers on his chin
And twinkling eyes and wrinkled skin
   And hair of palest yellow.
He wore a stovepipe hat of black,
A crimson cape upon his back,
And on his shoulder hung a sack:
   A most peculiar fellow.

"Let's let him try!" a voice cried out.
"We're in a pickle, there's no doubt!"
"Hear! Hear!" There soon rose up a shout.
    "Let's let the fellow try it!
We haven't anything to lose
Nor any other plans to choose;
And if this offer we refuse,
    We fear there'll be a riot!"

But just before they paid his fee,
The mayor spoke up. "Hold on!" said he.
"Although I do not wish to be
    A killjoy doubting Thomas,
Just hold your horses, if you will,
And let's not pay his bill until
A demonstration of his skill
    Proves he can keep his promise."

"Of course I'll prove it," said the man.
"I'll gladly show you that I can."
And from his pack he took a fan
    And waved it all around them.
And suddenly beneath each nose
The most bewitching smell arose:
The perfect perfume of a rose.
    The odor nearly drowned them.

The mayor sniffed in and out with bliss,
Each breath delicious as a kiss.
He'd never seen a fan like this.
    It was a fine invention.
"But though," he said, "the smell is nice,
I do not find it worth the price
Since why it will get rid of mice
    Escapes my comprehension."

The fellow answered in reply,
"Most honored sir, I'll show you why."
He took the fan and waved it high
    Until a breeze was lifted.
And suddenly throughout the space
The smell was gone without a trace,
And in a moment in its place
    Another odor drifted.

The mayor's wife wrinkled up her nose.
"What is that smell, do you suppose?
The more I sniff, the worse it grows.
    I fear it's getting stronger."
"Dear Madam," said the fellow, "please,
I beg you put your mind at ease.
Although this odor disagrees,
    It will not last much longer."

And when the townsfolk in dismay
Began to cough and turn away,
He cried, "Dear friends, I beg you stay!
    This odor cannot hurt you!
And though I know the smell is vile,
Just hold your noses for a while
And shut your mouths and do not smile
    Until your mice desert you."

Meanwhile through town and countryside,
In every mousehole far and wide,
Wherever rodents did reside,
    The miracle was squeaked of.
And all, however lame or stiff,
Ran out to catch a little sniff,
To snatch at least a tiny whiff
    Of what the region reeked of.

Some said it smelled of Brie from France,
While others swore 'twas Liederkranz
Or Gorgonzola, ripe, perchance,
    Or Stilton, Swiss, or Edam;
But all agreed that they would do
All that the man might ask them to
And they would follow in a queue
    Wherever he might lead 'em.

The townsfolk laughed; the children cheered;
The mayor was sorry he had sneered,
And all his doubts had disappeared.
    The chap was now their hero.
With gratitude their spirits soared,
Though when they paid him his reward
(Much larger than they could afford),
    Their bank accounts were zero.

He took his fee and off they went.
A most remarkable event!
And ever fainter grew the scent
    Until at last it vanished.
And all the people clapped and cheered
Because the air at last was cleared
And all the mice had disappeared,
    Forever to be banished.

O happy day! The mice were gone!
They celebrated till the dawn!
Then everyone began to yawn,
    And soon they all were sleeping.
But in the darkness while they slept,
Out of their houses creatures crept;
Along the silent streets they stepped,
    On padded paws went creeping.

And when the people woke, they found
Their cats had left without a sound;
Not even one was still around;
    They were without a feline!
And when their dogs discovered that,
They ran away in nothing flat,
For what's a dog without a cat?
    They took off in a beeline.

The children then began to whine,
"Although a mouseless town is fine,
At catless towns we draw the line,
And dogless towns are awful!

Without our pets we will not stay!
We cannot live a single day!"
And so the children ran away,
    Although it was not lawful.

This put the townsfolk in a state,
And one and all bemoaned their fate.
Their hearts were sad, their sorrow great;
    How could their children leave them?
But later when they understood
Their children had gone off for good,
They set off quickly as they could
    To find them and retrieve them.

But when at last they found the crowd,
The children all looked very proud
And told their parents they had vowed
    To stick by their decision.
"We do not mean to be unkind.
We hope and pray you do not mind;
But we can't leave our pets behind
    Without our supervision."

Meanwhile the chap who had begun
The whole affair, the very one,
Was lounging in the noonday sun,
    The odor even stronger;
And all around him danced the mice
Who'd cost the town so high a price
As if they lived in Paradise
    And craved the town no longer.

"You've led our children far astray,
And now they will not come away.
It's all your fault. What do you say?"
    The townsfolk all accused him.
He looked them over for a while,
Then smiled a secret little smile,
Rather like a crocodile,
    As if they all amused him.

"My dearest friends, don't be absurd!
Your mice are gone. I kept my word.
They might have stayed if you preferred.
    I kept my bargain, clearly.
I understand your deep concern;
You want your children to return;
But as you see, your words they spurn;
    They love their pets so dearly.

"And since the children won't go back
As long as cats and dogs they lack,
You'll have to try a different tack.
    Now let me lead you through it:
To lure the dogs, the cats must part;
To lure the cats, the mice must start;
To lure the mice . . . now that's an art!
    No one but I can do it!"

The fellow waved his fan. At that
The mice came running pitti-pat,
And after them came every cat
   And all the dogs thereafter.
And then the children, two by two,
Went marching down the avenue,
Exactly as he said they'd do,
   With merry peals of laughter.

And last in line, their hearts like lead,
The townsfolk trod with heavy tread
In dread of what lay up ahead:
    A *second* mouse invasion.
And also, floating in the breeze,
They'd have as well the smell of cheese!
The cure was worse than the disease!
    Oh, what a sad occasion!

$\mathcal{A}$nd when they finally reached their town
And all of them had settled down,
Their foreheads furrowed with a frown
    And hot beneath their collars,
The fellow told them if they'd pay,
He'd take the mice and go away
While making sure the cats would stay.
    The price? One hundred dollars.

"But, sir, we've no more money now!"
The mayor explained with wrinkled brow.
"We'd pay you but we don't know how!"
    It was a great disaster.
They had no way to meet the cost.
With no more money all was lost.
The fellow's heart seemed cold as frost.
    He had become their master.

But as he stood there, tall and proud,
Observing the unhappy crowd,
A piping voice spoke clear and loud,
    "I've thought of a solution!"
It was a little girl who spoke.
They wondered if it was a joke,
Or could she really save the folk
    And end their persecution?

"While we've no money we can give,
He hasn't got a place to live;
And so I'm almost positive
    He'd pay *us* for a dwelling.
And if we build it out of brick
And make the walls extremely thick,
And if we build it double-quick,
    It soon will stop the smelling."

Her plan was good, they did agree;
But first of all they'd have to see
If he would pay them back his fee
    To buy a place to live in.
At first he said it wasn't fair.
Why, he could live most anywhere
Without a house. He did not care.
    He did not want to give in.

But when he started to recall
He hadn't had a home at all
Or anyplace that he could call
    His own since he was teeny
And how he'd suffered from that lack,
He took the money from his pack
And bowing low he paid them back,
    No longer such a meany.

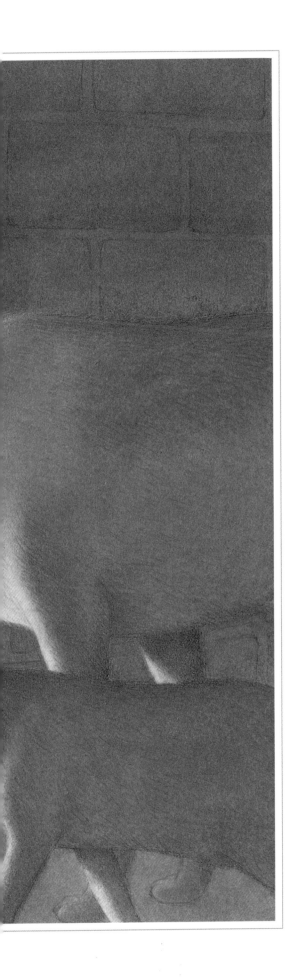

The townsfolk worked around the clock
And raised a structure block by block.
The house was solid as a rock
    And in it they installed him.
And as the night began to fall,
The mice arrived and filled the hall.
They cheered the Mouse Man, one and all
    (For that is what they called him).

And from that day to this, perhaps,
As dogs awaken from their naps,
The cats slip off their owners' laps,
    And off they all go gaily.
The house is less than half a mile.
The mice receive them with a smile.
And though they only stay awhile,
    They pay these visits daily.

And sometimes when the wind's increased
And blows directly from the east,
The townsfolk may detect the least
    Delicious scent of roses.
They know this is the Mouse Man's sign
Inviting them to come and dine,
And so they all march off in line
    Just following their noses.